PEANUTS®
Time for School,
CHARLIE BROWN

by Charles M. Schulz
adapted by Maggie Testa
illustrated by Robert Pope

Ready-to-Read

Simon Spotlight
New York London Toronto Sydney New Delhi

Poor Charlie Brown!
He can't kick a football.
Or throw a decent pitch.
Or even fly a kite.
But when it comes to
worrying about school,
he is the world champ!

"You look down, Charlie Brown,"
Linus says.

"I worry about school a lot,"
Charlie Brown replies.
"And then I worry about worrying
so much about school!"

Charlie Brown decides to get help.
"What's your problem?" Lucy asks.
"I worry about tomorrow."
Charlie Brown answers.
"Then when tomorrow becomes
today, I start worrying about
tomorrow again!"

"I think I can help you,"
Lucy tells Charlie Brown.
"What you need is confidence!"

"Throw out your chest
and face the future!" Lucy shouts.
"Now raise your arm
and clench your fist!"
Charlie Brown does what
Lucy tells him to do.
Suddenly Charlie Brown isn't
worried about school anymore!

He might ace every pop quiz!
He might become hall monitor!
He might even talk to the
Little Red-Haired Girl!
Lucy interrupts Charlie Brown's
daydream.
"You look ridiculous!" she says.

A few days after school starts,
the teacher tells the students about
the spelling bee.

Charlie Brown thinks
about entering it.
It could be good for him.
He could gain confidence.

Charlie Brown goes to raise his
hand to volunteer.
But his hand won't go up.
"My hand is smarter than I am,"
Charlie Brown groans.

Charlie Brown enters
the spelling bee anyway.
"You're crazy," Lucy whispers.
"Don't do it.
You'll just make a fool of yourself!"

Charlie Brown throws his hands
up in the air.
"I can try, can't I?"
Charlie Brown asks.

"What's the good of living if you don't try a few things?"

Lucy leans over again.
"Spell 'Acetylcholinesterase'!"
Charlie Brown gulps.

"Maybe I shouldn't have entered,"
he says.

But as the spelling bee
gets closer and closer,
Charlie Brown gets braver.
He feels more confident.
"Nobody thinks I can win, Snoopy,"
Charlie Brown tells his dog.
"But I'm going to show them."

"I do have trouble remembering some rules," Charlie Brown admits. "'I' before 'B' except after 'T'? Is it 'V' before 'Z' except after 'E'?" *Good grief*, thinks Snoopy!

It is the day of the spelling bee.
Charlie Brown feels calm.
He feels confident.

All the words in the first round
are easy, he thinks.

Soon it is Charlie Brown's turn.
"Maze?" he repeats
after the teacher gives him the
word.

Charlie Brown isn't worried.
He smiles. He takes a deep breath.
He begins to spell.
"M-A-Y-S!"

Charlie Brown blows it!
Soon he is back at his desk and he
is worrying.
What will his friends say?
What will Snoopy do?

"Yes, ma'am?" Charlie Brown answers when his teacher calls his name.
"Why did I have my head on my desk?"

"Because I blew the spelling bee!"
Charlie Brown yells.
"That's why!"
Charlie Brown covers his mouth
with his hands.
Yelling at the teacher is
never a good idea!

"Oh, good grief!" he says.
It is the worst day
of Charlie Brown's life.
He woke up looking forward
to the spelling bee.
And he ended up
in the principal's office.

"On a day like this, a person really needs his faithful dog to come running out to greet him!" Charlie Brown says on his walk home.

Snoopy is there waiting for Charlie
Brown when he gets home.

Happiness is a warm puppy.

Poor Charlie Brown!
He can't kick a football.
Or throw a decent pitch.
Or even fly a kite.
But at least he has Snoopy!

Charlie Brown is never happier than
when he's with Snoopy.
"What a pair!" Lucy says.

PEANUTS®
Make a Trade,
CHARLIE BROWN!

by Charles M. Schulz
adapted by Tina Gallo
illustrated by Robert Pope

Ready-to-Read

Simon Spotlight
New York London Toronto Sydney New Delhi

This is Charlie Brown.
He's the manager of a
baseball team.
They have never won a game.
He needs to make a change!

Lucy is the worst player
on the team.
"I'm thinking of making some
changes," Charlie Brown says.
"What kind of changes?" Lucy asks.

"I'm going to trade some players,"
Charlie Brown tells her.
"A few trades can make our team
much better."
"That's a great idea," Lucy says.
"Why don't you trade yourself?"

Charlie Brown calls Peppermint Patty.
"Would you like to trade
any players?" he asks.
"I don't know, Chuck," she says.
"The only good player you have
is the little kid with the big nose."

"You mean Snoopy?" Charlie Brown
says. "Oh no, I was thinking
more of Lucy."
Charlie Brown hears a click.
Peppermint Patty has hung up!

The next day Charlie Brown tells
Linus about the phone call.
"Peppermint Patty only wants
Snoopy. I told her no, but maybe
I was wrong."

Linus is surprised.
"You would trade your own dog just to win a few ball games?" he said.
Charlie Brown's eyes grew wide.
"Win!" he said. "Have you ever noticed what a beautiful word that is? Win! Win! Win!"

The next day Charlie Brown calls
Peppermint Patty.
"I'll trade Snoopy," he says.
"Great!" Peppermint Patty says.
"I'll give you five players
for Snoopy. It's a deal."

Charlie Brown hangs up the phone.
*Good grief! I've traded away
my own dog*, Charlie Brown thinks.
I've become a real manager!

Peppermint Patty has the contract
ready for Charlie Brown to sign.
Charlie Brown is nervous.
"Try not to let your hand shake
so much when you sign the
contract, Chuck!"
Peppermint Patty says.

Charlie Brown has to tell Snoopy.
"This is hard for me to say. I've
traded you for five new players.
Please don't hate me, Snoopy."
"Bleah!" Snoopy responds.

Charlie Brown tells Schroeder the news. Schroeder is shocked.
"You traded your own dog?" he said.
"Does winning a ball game mean that much to you?"
"I don't know, I've never won a ball game," Charlie Brown replies.

Linus is upset.
"I don't even want to talk
to you, Charlie Brown," he says.
Charlie Brown doesn't say a word.
"And stop breathing on my
blanket!" Linus yells.

Charlie Brown runs back
to Snoopy's doghouse.
"I was wrong," he says to
Snoopy. "I could never trade you!"
"Look! The deal is off." He rips
up the contract in front of Snoopy.

Suddenly, Peppermint Patty
appears at his side.
She sees the ripped-up contract.
"I guess you got my message,
Chuck,"
she says. "The deal is off."

"Those players said they would quit baseball before they played on your team. Sorry, Chuck. I hope you're not too angry," Peppermint Patty said.

"I'm crushed," Charlie Brown says.
But he doesn't really mean it.
He's thrilled! So is Snoopy!
Snoopy is so happy he
starts dancing!

Meanwhile, Peppermint Patty has
a problem with her team too.
Marcie is her right fielder.
She is as bad as Lucy!
"I hate baseball!" Marcie shouts.

Peppermint Patty calls
Charlie Brown with an idea.
"I'll trade you Marcie for Lucy,"
she says.
"Great!" Charlie Brown says.
"I'll trade Lucy for anyone!"

"You traded me for Marcie?" Lucy says. "You made a terrible deal. Marcie is awful."
"No, it's a good deal," Charlie Brown says. "Peppermint Patty threw in a pizza!"

Marcie loves being on Charlie Brown's team. There is just one problem. She never leaves the pitcher's mound. She likes being close to Charlie Brown!

"Marcie, you're supposed to be in right field," Charlie Brown says. "I'm happier when I'm near you, Charles," Marcie tells him. "I've always been fond of you."

Lucy isn't working out for
Peppermint Patty either.
"Just keep your eye on the ball,"
she tells Lucy.
So Lucy stares at the ball in
Peppermint Patty's hand.

"It's hard to keep my eye on the ball when you keep moving it around," Lucy says.
Later that night Peppermint Patty calls Charlie Brown. "You need to take Lucy back, Chuck!" Peppermint Patty says.

"Why?" asks Charlie Brown.
"Lucy's the worst player I've ever
had," Peppermint Patty tells him.
"But I already ate the pizza!"
Charlie Brown says.

Charlie Brown tells Marcie she's
been traded back to
Peppermint Patty's team.
Marcie is sad the deal is over.

"I guess I wasn't much help,"
Marcie says to Charlie Brown.
"I didn't score a single goal."
Charlie Brown doesn't bother
telling Marcie goals are in
soccer, not baseball!

It's Lucy's first game back
on Charlie Brown's team.
She's holding an umbrella
over her head. A ball bounces
off the umbrella.

"It's not even raining!" shouts
Charlie Brown.
"Not yet," Lucy says.
Suddenly it starts to pour!
The entire team runs for cover,
except for Charlie Brown.

Charlie Brown is getting soaked, but he doesn't care. His team is back together, and they can't lose the game—it's a rainout!

PEANUTS®

You Got a Rock, CHARLIE BROWN!

by Charles M. Schulz
adapted by Maggie Testa
illustrated by Robert Pope

Ready-to-Read

Simon Spotlight
New York   London   Toronto   Sydney   New Delhi

The leaves are changing colors
and falling from the trees.
There's a chill in the air.
There are pumpkins all around.
It's Halloween!
Charlie Brown loves Halloween.

Tonight, Charlie Brown is going
trick-or-treating.

First he needs to figure out
what to wear.

Charlie Brown decides to dress up
as a ghost.
It should be an easy costume
to make.
All he needs to do is cut two
eyeholes out of a sheet.

Charlie Brown meets up
with his friends.
"Really, Charlie Brown, what are
you supposed to be?" asks Lucy.
"A ghost," Charlie Brown replies.
"I guess I had a little trouble
with the scissors."

Lucy is dressed up as a witch.

"A person should always pick
a costume which is in direct contrast
to one's own personality," she says.

Someone else dressed up
as a ghost joins the group.
"Hi, Pigpen," says Frieda.

"How did you know it was me?"
Pigpen asks.
Even a sheet can't cover the
cloud of dirt that always
surrounds Pigpen!

Snoopy is also in the
Halloween spirit.
He wears a red scarf, goggles,
and a green cap.

"It's the World War One Flying Ace,"
explains Charlie Brown.
"Now I've heard everything!"
says Lucy.

Time for trick-or-treating!
The group of friends walks
to the first house.
Lucy rings the doorbell.

"Trick or treat," everyone shouts
when the door opens.
Everyone gets a little something
in his or her bag.

On the way to the next house,
everyone compares their treats.
"I got five pieces of candy,"
says Lucy.

"I got a chocolate bar,"
says Violet.
"I got a quarter,"
says Pigpen.

Charlie Brown looks in his bag.
He can't believe his eyes.
"I got a rock," he moans.

The group goes to the next house.
"Trick or treat," everyone shouts
when the door opens.
Once again, everyone gets a little
something in his or her bag.

"I got a candy bar,"
says Lucy.

"I got three cookies,"
says Violet.

"I got a pack of gum,"
says Pigpen.

Charlie Brown looks in his bag.
"I got a rock," says Charlie Brown.
"Not again!"

Charlie Brown hopes things will be
different at the next house.
"Trick or treat," everyone shouts
when the door opens.

"I got a popcorn ball," says Lucy.
"I got a fudge bar," says Violet.

Charlie Brown looks in his bag.
This time, he is not surprised.
"I got a rock," he tells everyone.

After trick-or-treating,
Charlie Brown and his bag of rocks
go to Violet's Halloween party.
Lucy asks if Charlie Brown wants to
be a model.

Charlie Brown is honored,
but not for long.
Lucy only wants to draw
a face on the back of his head.
"Thank you, Charlie Brown,"
says Lucy.
"You made an excellent model."

The next day, Charlie Brown tells
Linus all about the night before.

"Another Halloween has come and gone and all I got was a bag full of rocks," he says.

At least there's always next year!

PEANUTS®

LUCY
Knows Best

PSYCHIATRIC
HELP 5¢

THE DOCTOR
IS IN

by Charles M. Schulz

adapted by Kama Einhorn

illustrated by Robert Pope

Ready-to-Read

Simon Spotlight
New York   London   Toronto   Sydney   New Delhi

Lucy has a booth where
she helps friends with their
problems. Lucy gives lots of
advice, and it only
costs five cents!

Charlie Brown is Lucy's biggest
customer.
"Why are you so good at
helping people?" he asks.

Charlie Brown wants to feel
confident, like Lucy.
"Try whistling," Lucy says.
"You'll feel better about
yourself and everyone around you."

Charlie Brown walks home,
whistling. He feels better!
Then he passes Woodstock,
whistling a fancier tune.
Charlie Brown stops whistling.
He doesn't feel as good
about himself anymore.

Charlie Brown goes back to Lucy.
"I think I need another suggestion,"
he says.
"You're hopeless," she says. "Next!"

"Will you help my dog, Snoopy?
He can't sleep because he's afraid of
the dark," says Charlie Brown.
"I'll help anyone with five cents!"
Lucy says.

Snoopy comes to see Lucy.
"The dark can't hurt you,"
says Lucy.
Snoopy falls asleep at the booth!
"Stay awake when I'm talking
to you!" screams Lucy.

"Give me your paw,"
Lucy says. "Say to yourself:
I am loved. I am needed.
I am important."
Snoopy feels better holding Lucy's
hand. He smiles!
Lucy sends him home.

At home Snoopy finds Woodstock.
Woodstock looks sad.
Snoopy knows what to do!

Snoopy brings Woodstock to see
Lucy.
"Good grief! Why are you so
mopey?" she says. "You're a bird!
You can fly! Remember . . .
there's a great big sky out there!"

THE DOCTOR

Lucy is right! Woodstock flaps
his little wings and takes off.
"Rats!" Lucy says. "I helped
him so fast, he flew
away without paying!"

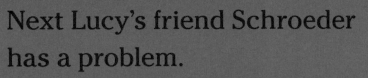

Next Lucy's friend Schroeder
has a problem.
"I want to go to summer music
camp, but I don't know how
to get there," he says.

THE DOCTOR
IS IN

Lucy thinks Schroeder is cute.
She helps him really quickly.
"I've booked you on flight
fifty-four, first class!" she says,
handing him a ticket.

"Wow," Schroeder says. "You
are so helpful."
"Yes, I'll even kiss you
good-bye!" Lucy says.

Lucy leans in for a kiss,
but Schroeder ignores her.
"I have to look for a magazine
to read on the plane," he says.

Lucy is disappointed.
When Schroeder comes back
from camp, she tries again
to get his attention.

"I read that our arms weren't made for throwing baseballs," Lucy says. "Really?" Schroeder asks. "What are arms made for?"

"Hugging!" Lucy grins.
Schroeder rolls his eyes
and says, "BLEAH!"

Ugh! Lucy is angry with Schroeder. She stomps home to sulk. She crawls into her beanbag chair and sinks all the way down. She needs advice. Who can she ask?

Herself!
Lucy goes to her own booth.
"I need some help," she says out
loud.

Then Lucy moves behind the booth. "Good. That's why I'm here," she answers.

Lucy moves to the other
side of the booth. "There's this
boy I like, but he never notices me,"
she says.
"It makes me sad."

Lucy moves behind the booth
again. "What's the problem?" she
asks. "You're smart and beautiful.
You shouldn't chase after anyone!"

"Do you really think so?"
Lucy asks.
"Of course!" she says from behind
the booth. "I wouldn't lie to you!"
That's just what Lucy needs to hear!

She walks straight to Schroeder's
house.
On the way she thinks about how
smart she is. She fixes everyone's
problems. Crummy old Schroeder
only cares about his music.

"I got advice from the smartest
person I know. Want to know
what she said?" Lucy asks.
Schroeder ignores her.
Lucy sticks out her tongue.
"She said . . . BLEAH!"